This book belongs to:

No Buddy Like a Book

Allan Wolf

illustrated by Brianne Farley

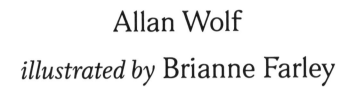

CANDLEWICK PRESS

"port"
"starboard"

WE learn important stuff from books.
We learn to speak and think.

We learn why icebergs stay afloat . . .
and why *Titanic*s sink.

We learn to play harmonica.
We learn to bake and cook.
We learn to read and write.
There is no buddy like a book.

But books are only smears of ink
without the reader's mind
to give the letters meaning
and to read between the lines.

So step aboard the Book Express.
It's waiting at the station.
But can you guess the address
of your final destination?

The greatest nation in the world:

your own imagination!

I've learned to name the planets
and to track a distant star.
I've learned to bottle moonlight
and to calculate how far

a solid rocket booster sends
a shuttle into space.
I learned to build a telescope
to see space face-to-face.

This homemade pinhole viewer
even lets me see the sun.
There is no buddy like a book
to show you how it's done.

1.

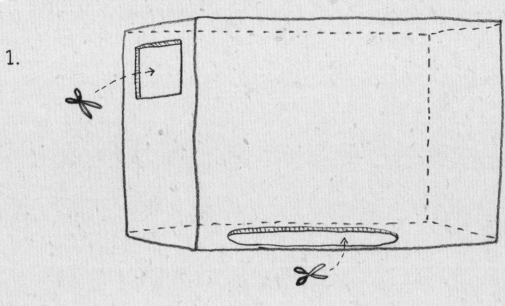

2.

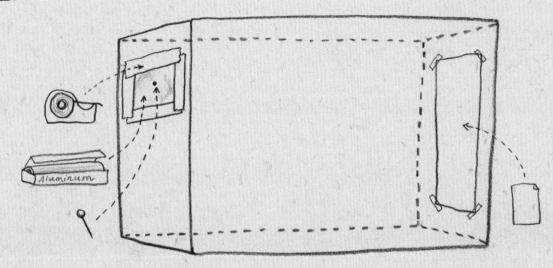

3.

My launchpad is a science book.
My mind's a constellation.
The only rocket fuel I need
is my own imagination.

I've climbed the heights of Everest,
one hand behind my back.
I've seen the sights of India
from high atop a yak.

I've anteloped in Africa
and kissed a crocodile
as I was sailing all alone
along the river Nile.

I'm quite the global traveler.
I've been to every land:
China, England, Russia, Rome,
New Guinea, and Sudan.

New Zealand and Australia,
Yugoslavia and Perth.
Canada and Kathmandu.
Dallas and Fort Worth.

SCARLET MACAW
HONDURAS

RAGGIANA
BIRD-OF-PARADISE
PAPUA NEW GUINEA

MOCKINGBIRD
UNITED STATES

SPINDALIS
PUERTO RICO

SPARROW
ITALY

EUROPEAN ROBIN
UNITED KINGDOM

NIGHTINGALE
CROATIA

AMERICAN ROBIN
UNITED STATES

RED-CROWNED CRANE
CHINA

RUFOUS HORNERO
ARGENTINA

EMU
AUSTRALIA

KIWI
NEW ZEALAND

But although these wondrous places hold
a certain fascination,
the greatest nation in the world
is my own imagination!

I visit any world I wish
and never leave my chair.
There is no buddy like a book
to make me feel I'm there.

So step aboard the Book Express.
It's leaving from the station.
The only ticket needed is
your own imagination.

Whatever are you waiting for?
The adventure starts today.
Just grab a book from off the shelf . . .

and you're on your way.

For Peter, Kaye, and Sarah Graham—
the best book buddies ever!
AW

To Ruth, to Dasha, to Peter, to Thyra,
and, always, to Jon
BF

First edition 2021

Library of Congress Catalog Card Number pending
ISBN 978-1-5362-0307-3

20 21 22 23 24 25 CCP 10 9 8 7 6 5 4 3 2 1

Printed in Shenzhen, Guangdong, China

This book was typeset in My Happy 70s.
The illustrations were done in gouache, colored pencil, charcoal,
wax pastel, and glue on mulberry paper and watercolor paper.

Candlewick Press
99 Dover Street
Somerville, Massachusetts 02144

www.candlewick.com